BON

BL N/A
PTS N/A

D1084044

PEAS
AND
HONEY

Written and Compiled by
KIMBERLY COLEN

Illustrated by
MANDY VICTOR

Wordsong
BOYDS MILLS PRESS

PEAS
AND
HONEY

RECIPES FOR KIDS
(WITH A PINCH OF POETRY)

To Dad, who nurtured my love of culture.
To Mom, who inspired my passion for
cooking—K.C.

To Bill, Chris, and Jeff, with love—M.V.

Text copyright © 1995 by Kimberly Colen
Illustrations copyright © 1995 by Mandy Victor

Published by Wordsong
Boyds Mills Press, Inc.
A Highlights Company
815 Church Street
Honesdale, Pennsylvania 18431
Printed in Mexico

Publisher Cataloging-in-Publication Data
Colen, Kimberly.
Peas and honey : recipes for kids (with a pinch of poetry) /
written and compiled by Kimberly Colen ;
illustrated by Mandy Victor.—1st ed.
[64]p. : col. ill. ; cm.
Includes index.
Summary : Recipes to make cookies, omelets, muffins, and more.
Also includes poems, food facts,
and the poets' own memories about food.
ISBN 1-56397-062-7
1. Cookery—Juvenile literature. 2. Food—Juvenile poetry. 3. Children's poetry.
[1. Cookery. 2. Food—Poetry. 3. Poetry.]
I. Victor, Mandy, ill.
II. Title.
641.5—dc20   1995   CIP
Library of Congress Catalog Card Number 91-68052

First edition, 1995
Book designed by Katy Riegel
The text of this book is set in 11-point Adobe Garamond.
The illustrations are done in colored pencil.
Distributed by St. Martin's Press

1   3   5   7   9   10   8   6   4   2

TABLE OF CONTENTS

WHAT'S INSIDE

THIS BOOK IS full of poetry. It's also a cookbook packed with recipes, fantastic food facts, cooking tips, and some of the poets' own memories about food.

One of the most important ways to use this book is to share it. Memorize a poem and recite it as you present the meal. Ask an adult to help you in the kitchen, then cook up a specialty for them. Read a poem to friends or family, then tell them an interesting fact about the same food.

Be sure your kitchen is always a safe place to work. Read "Cooking in a Safe Kitchen" on page 8 before you begin, and stick to the rules. They're meant to help you become a good cook. Also, follow the directions for each recipe. You'll get the best and tastiest results that way.

This book doesn't really end, even after you finish reading. You have poems to remember, cooking to do, and discoveries to share. Enjoy yourself as you bring together poems, food, and friends in the pages that follow.

COOKING IN A SAFE KITCHEN

1. Read recipes all the way through before you begin. Carefully watch what you are cooking.
2. Get out all utensils and ingredients before you begin a recipe.
3. Ask an older person for help if you don't understand something.
4. When using knives, point the blade away from you. Cut on a solid cutting board. Do not touch the blade. If you drop a knife, don't try to catch it. Let it drop before you pick it up. Be sure to wash it off before using it again.
5. When using a blender, plug it in with dry hands. After you are finished using it, unplug it with dry hands. Put on the lid before you turn on the machine. Never put your fingers inside the blender while it is running.
6. If you grate food, be careful of your fingers and knuckles. (Always point the grating side away from you.)
7. Use potholders to remove something from the stove or oven. Make sure pot holders are dry—wet ones let the heat through.
8. When you are finished using the stove, turn it off.
9. Turn the handles of pans to the side so you won't knock them over. Keep them away from other hot burners.
10. Remove spoons from hot pans. Metal spoons get hot and plastic spoons can melt.
11. Be careful when draining food (like spaghetti). The steam can burn.
12. The lids of just-opened cans have sharp edges that you should avoid touching. Use a table knife to lift the lid, and then hold the lid in the middle when throwing it away.
13. If you drop something on the floor, clean it up right away so the floor doesn't become slippery.

A COOK'S TOOLS

Some poets work with pencil and paper and some work with a word processor. But to complete the job a poet must have certain tools. A cook also needs certain tools to complete a job. To prepare a recipe, measuring cups, spoons, mixing bowls, and other equipment are necessary. On the next two pages, you'll find most of the tools you need to complete the recipes in the book.

UTENSILS

paring knife   table knife   wooden spoon

spatula   fork   vegetable peeler

measuring spoons   bread knife   grater

measuring cup   rubber scraper   electric mixer/hand beater

mixing spoon   can opener   pastry brush

POTS AND PANS

skillet

cookie sheet

muffin pan

1, 2, and 3-quart saucepans

pie plate

frying pan

small baking dish

MISCELLANEOUS

cutting board

mixing bowls

potholders

colander

sifter

blender

THROUGH THE TEETH

Through the teeth
And past the gums
Look out stomach,
Here it comes!

Folk Rhyme

Yaaaawwwn. Strrrretch. Start off the new day at your best. Roll out of bed and into the kitchen. Crack open an egg, drop a slice of bread in the toaster, put a fresh batch of muffins into the oven, and smell the aromas of morning.

Breakfast feeds your body and poetry nourishes your soul. Open your eyes and celebrate both.

FRUITS

Currants on a bush,
And figs upon a stem,
And cherries on a bending bough,
And Ned to gather them.

Christina G. Rossetti

AN EGG

I wonder how
an egg's begun.
The yolk
is yellow as the sun.
The color of the white
is . . . none.
You'd think the yolk
and white would run
before the shell
was ever done . . .
But hens don't lay
a scrambled one!

Aileen Fisher

COOKING TIP

To test an egg for freshness, put the entire egg—with shell—in
a bowl filled with warm water. Fresh eggs sink to the bottom;
rotten eggs float to the top.

BASIC OMELET

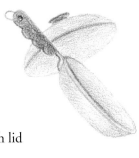

INGREDIENTS

2 eggs
1 tablespoon cold water
salt and pepper (optional)
butter or oil or non-stick
    cooking spray

UTENSILS

cutting board
paring knife
small bowl
mixing spoon
7-inch skillet with lid
spatula

Fillings: shredded cheese, sliced mushrooms, onions, ham, salami, cooked and crumbled bacon, diced tomato

Sweet Fillings: sliced strawberries, kiwi, bananas, shredded coconut, chopped nuts, sour cream, brown sugar

STEPS

1. Cut up fillings of your choice on a cutting board. Set aside.
2. Break eggs into small bowl and add water. Salt and pepper also may be added, if desired. Mix well with mixing spoon.
3. Place skillet over medium-high heat. Cover bottom and sides of skillet with butter or oil. Or coat inside of skillet with non-stick cooking spray.
4. Add egg mixture to skillet. As omelet cooks, use spatula to lift edges of cooked egg. Tilt skillet so that uncooked portion runs underneath the sides. Continue lifting and tilting until top side is no longer runny.
5. Spread fillings onto one half of egg mixture and turn heat to low. Cover and let eggs cook another minute.
6. Remove lid. Loosen half of the omelet and fold it over the other half. Remove skillet from stove and slide omelet onto a plate.

Makes 1 serving.

MORE PANCAKES

A hundred million pancakes,
I'd like to have to eat;
I'd spread them thick with butter
And pour on syrup sweet.

A hundred million pancakes,
How good they all would taste;
I'd eat them fast as lightning,
With not a one to waste!

Lois Lenski

WORLD'S BIGGEST PANCAKE

The biggest pancake ever cooked was in the Netherlands. It was 32 feet long, 11 inches wide and 1 inch thick. It weighed 2,866 pounds!

YOGURT WHOLE WHEAT PANCAKES

INGREDIENTS

1 1/2 cups whole wheat flour
3 tablespoons baking powder
1/2 teaspoon salt
1 1/2 cups plain yogurt
3 eggs
1 1/2 teaspoons honey
3 tablespoons oil
butter or margarine or non-stick
   cooking spray

UTENSILS

measuring cup
measuring spoons
2 mixing bowls
mixing spoon
7-inch skillet
spatula

STEPS

1. Mix flour, baking powder, and salt in one mixing bowl.
2. In another mixing bowl, add yogurt, eggs, honey, and oil. Mix until smooth. Combine flour and yogurt mixtures and stir until all ingredients are well blended.
3. Melt two tablespoons of butter or margarine in skillet over medium heat. Tilt skillet as butter or margarine melts until the inside is hot and well greased. Or coat inside of skillet with non-stick cooking spray.
4. Pour one tablespoon of mixture into hot skillet. Flip pancake when holes start to bubble through, then flatten with spatula. Cook until both sides are brown. Remove pancake from skillet and serve.
5. Grease or spray pan each time you add more pancake mixture so that pancakes won't stick. Serve warm.

Makes about 12-18 3-inch pancakes.

COOKING TIP

- After you mix the pancake batter, let it stand for one hour. This makes the batter fluffy and your pancakes more tender.
- To make sure the skillet is hot enough, sprinkle some water inside. If the drops bounce around and then evaporate, the skillet is ready.

YELLOW BUTTER

Yellow butter purple jelly red jam black bread

Spread it thick
Say it quick

Yellow butter purple jelly red jam black bread

Spread it thicker
Say it quicker

Yellow butter purple jelly red jam black bread

Now repeat it
While you eat it

Yellow butter purple jelly red jam black bread

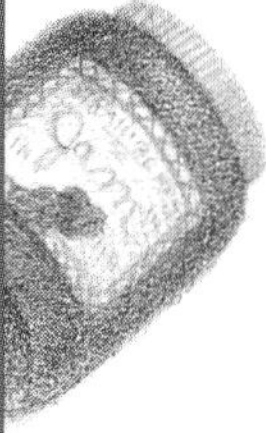

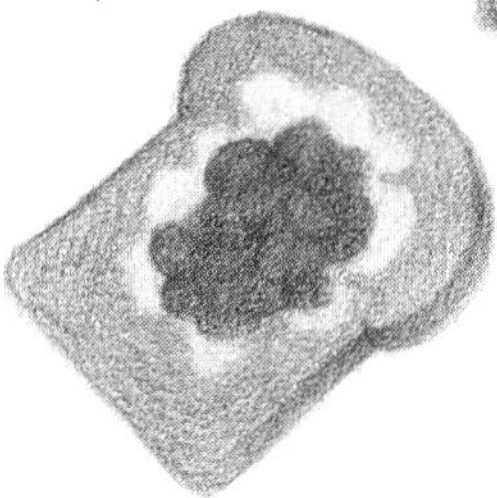

Don't talk
With your mouth full!

Mary Ann Hoberman

A tongue twister that fills your mouth with delicious words!
I've always loved butter—my mother always says that I ate
bread on butter, I consumed so much of it!

Mary Ann Hoberman

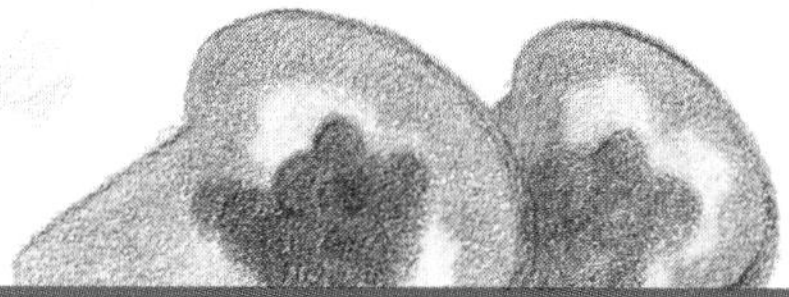

FRUITY-CHEESY TOAST

INGREDIENTS

slice of whole wheat bread
butter or margarine
1/4 cup low-fat cottage cheese
1 tablespoon raisins
1/4 apple, peach, or pear
cinnamon

UTENSILS

table knife
small spoon
measuring cup
measuring spoons
paring knife
cookie sheet
potholders
spatula

STEPS

1. Preheat oven to broil setting.
2. Butter bread lightly on one side and toast it.
3. Spread cottage cheese on toast with small spoon.
4. Add raisins.
5. Slice apple or other fruit into very thin pieces. Place sliced fruit over raisins and sprinkle with cinnamon.
6. Set toast on cookie sheet and put into oven. Broil for 4-5 minutes. Remove cookie sheet from oven with potholders. Lift toast carefully with spatula and eat warm.

Makes 1 serving.

MUFFINS

When Mother
baked some muffins,
they got cracks
in all their stuffins
and their heads
puffed up with puffins
north and south,

And she called
them RAGAmuffins,
but the name
was full of bluffins,
for I couldn't
get ENUFFINS
in my mouth!

Aileen Fisher

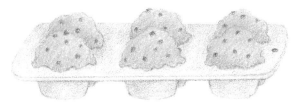

I was always happy when my mother baked muffins. I would break them open, hot from the oven, and hide a pat of butter inside to melt into the cracks and crevices. I liked them when I was young, and I still think that nuffin's better than muffins!

Aileen Fisher

MUFFINS WITH SURPRISE

INGREDIENTS

1 3/4 cups all-purpose flour
1/4 cup sugar
2 1/2 teaspoons baking powder
1 egg
3/4 cup milk
1/3 cup cooking oil
jelly or jam
powdered sugar

UTENSILS

muffin pan
paper bake cups
measuring cup
measuring spoons
large mixing bowl
small mixing bowl
fork
mixing spoon
damp cloth
potholders

STEPS

1. Preheat oven to 400°. Put one paper bake cup into each muffin cup.
2. In large mixing bowl, combine flour, sugar, and baking powder. Use mixing spoon to stir.
3. In small mixing bowl, beat egg. Add milk and oil. Beat mixture with fork until blended.
4. Add milk and egg mixture to flour mixture and stir with mixing spoon just until flour is moistened. Batter will look lumpy.
5. Spoon batter into muffin baking cups, filling each 1/3 full.
6. Put one teaspoon of jelly or jam in center of batter in each cup. Then fill muffin cups 2/3 full with remaining batter. Before baking, use damp cloth to wipe off spilled batter on muffin pan.
7. Bake for 20-25 minutes or until muffins are golden brown.
8. Remove muffins from oven with potholders. Sprinkle muffins with powdered sugar. Let cool.

Makes 12 muffins.

COOKING TIP

- Stir the batter just long enough for it to be lumpy. If you stir too long, the muffins will be tough.
- When testing the muffins for doneness, stick a toothpick in the center of one. If the toothpick comes out clean, they're ready. If not, keep them in the oven a while longer.
- Top off your muffin with one of these spreads: butter, cashew butter, almond butter, cream cheese, honey, maple syrup, grape jelly, strawberry jelly, apricot jelly, or marmalade.

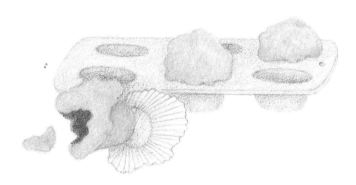

Any time is a good time to eat a sandwich, and you don't have to be a gourmet cook to prepare something delicious. Sandwiches are convenient and satisfying.

Like a poem, a sandwich is limited only by your imagination. Start with the first layer and add one line, one morsel on top of another. Create variations of your own.

IF THE MOON WERE MADE OF CHEESE

If the moon were made of cheese
I would reach into the sky
For a late-night snacking sandwich
Of ham and moon on rye.

Jeff Moss

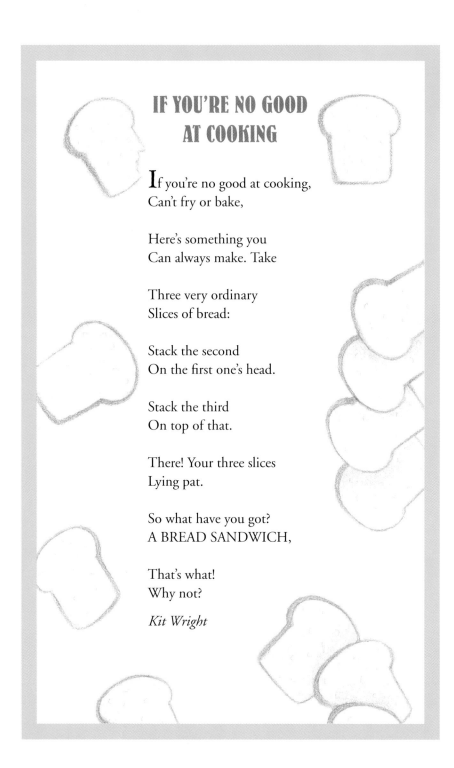

IF YOU'RE NO GOOD
AT COOKING

If you're no good at cooking,
Can't fry or bake,

Here's something you
Can always make. Take

Three very ordinary
Slices of bread:

Stack the second
On the first one's head.

Stack the third
On top of that.

There! Your three slices
Lying pat.

So what have you got?
A BREAD SANDWICH,

That's what!
Why not?

Kit Wright

HAM AND CHEESE ACCORDION SANDWICH

INGREDIENTS

16-inch loaf of French
   bread, sliced*
1/4 cup mayonnaise or
   salad dressing
2 teaspoons dried parsley flakes
2 teaspoons prepared mustard
1/2 teaspoon onion powder
8 slices of your favorite cheese
8 slices cooked ham

UTENSILS

bread knife
measuring cup
measuring spoons
mixing spoon
small mixing bowl
table knife
aluminum foil
potholders

STEPS

*Or cut unsliced loaf with bread knife into 15 even cuts, each 1 inch apart, slicing almost, but not quite through, the bread. Makes 16 equal slices.

1. Preheat oven to 375°.
2. Combine mayonnaise or salad dressing, dried parsley flakes, mustard, and onion powder in small bowl and stir together. With table knife, spread mixture into every other opening in bread.
3. Put one cheese slice on top of one ham slice and fold opposite corners together, making triangles. Insert ham and cheese into openings with mixture. Repeat with all cheese and ham slices.
4. Press loaf together and wrap tightly in aluminum foil. Bake in oven for 25-30 minutes or until hot. Use potholders to take loaf from oven.
5. Carefully remove foil. Cut unfilled openings through bottom crusts.

Makes 8 sandwiches.

WHERE'S THE DOUGH?

You've probably heard someone say, "Where's the dough?" That's because the words "bread" and "dough" have been used as slang words for "money."

Six thousand years ago, before coins were invented, people were paid in bags of grain or loaves of bread. Imagine getting an allowance of two slices of bread!

More than two hundred years ago, the sandwich was discovered by the fourth Earl of Sandwich. He was playing cards and didn't want to interrupt his game by eating, so he ordered his food to be served between two slices of bread. After that, the sandwich was born—and guess who it was named after!

(Actually, the Arabs have been filling pita bread pockets with food for centuries, and the Hebrews have been eating nuts, apples, and herbs between matzo for more than two thousand years.)

THE PERFECT TURKEY SANDWICH

Is my craving so outlandish
For the perfect turkey sandwich?
All white meat sliced sweet and thin
Mayonnaise to soak it in
Crispy lettuce for the flavor
Well spread butter for its savor
Salt and pepper now, to taste
There won't be a crumb to waste
Sometimes in my sleep I sigh
Turkey sandwich please on rye.

Steven Kroll

When I was growing up in New York City, the C & L Delicatessen on Broadway and 74th Street made the best turkey sandwich ever. Since then, turkey has always been my favorite sandwich. One day, walking past a deli on Madison Avenue, I was reminded of the C & L and decided to write a poem about that sandwich! If I were writing it today, however, I'd leave out all that high-cholesterol mayonnaise and butter, and substitute mustard.

Steven Kroll

"Peanut butter, considered as a spread . . . "
"How else could you consider it, my friend?"
"Well, by the spoonful; or, if sick in bed,
By licking it from the index finger's end."

David McCord

PEANUT BUTTER

INGREDIENTS

2 tablespoons oil
   (peanut or vegetable)
1 cup salted roasted peanuts
1-2 tablespoons honey

UTENSILS

measuring spoons
measuring cup
blender
rubber scraper
medium bowl
8-ounce capped jar

STEPS

1. Pour oil into blender.
2. Add peanuts.
3. Place top on blender and turn on to medium speed until peanuts are chopped into small pieces. Stop blender. Use scraper to push peanut pieces from sides of blender to bottom. Blend again until peanuts and oil are smooth and spreadable. You may need to add 1/2 teaspoon oil and blend a little longer.
4. Spoon peanut butter into bowl. Add honey, a little at a time, until peanut butter tastes right to you.
5. Serve fresh or store in 8-ounce capped jar. Keep in refrigerator.

VARIATIONS

- Chop a dozen peanuts into tiny pieces and add them to freshly made peanut butter for a chunky variation.

DINNER WINNERS

When was the last time you cooked dinner? Well, what about tonight! A good meal gives everyone a boost of energy after a hard day at work or a tough day in school.

Add freshly cut greenery to the center of the table, and recite a poem before you serve the meal—two simple touches you can share with those who are special.

When I was a kid, I loved spaghetti—it was delicious. My little brother and I used to do amazing things with it—like throw it at the ceiling and wait for it to fall. Sometimes we wore it like headbands or neckties. We'd even use a strand of spaghetti like a whip or lasso and try to catch a bug with it. I don't do those things anymore, but I do eat it with lots of sauce and cheese.

Jack Prelutsky

SPAGHETTI! SPAGHETTI!

Spaghetti! spaghetti!
you're wonderful stuff,
I love you, spaghetti,
I can't get enough.
You're covered with sauce
and you're sprinkled with cheese,
spaghetti! spaghetti!
oh, give me some please.

Spaghetti! spaghetti!
piled high in a mound,
you wiggle, you wriggle,
you squiggle around.
There's slurpy spaghetti
all over my plate,
spaghetti! spaghetti!
I think you are great.

Spaghetti! spaghetti!
I love you a lot,
you're slishy, you're sloshy,
delicious and hot.
I gobble you down
oh, I can't get enough,
spaghetti! spaghetti!
you're wonderful stuff.

Jack Prelutsky

CHEESY SPAGHETTI AND MEAT PIE

INGREDIENTS

water
6 ounces spaghetti
1/4 teaspoon salt
2 eggs
1/3 cup grated Parmesan cheese
2 tablespoons butter or margarine
non-stick cooking spray
1/2 pound lean ground beef
1 small onion
8 ounces of spaghetti sauce
3 slices of mozzarella cheese

UTENSILS

3-quart saucepan
measuring spoons
fork
colander
small mixing bowl
large mixing bowl
mixing spoon
9-inch pie plate
cutting board
sharp knife

STEPS

1. Fill 3-quart saucepan halfway with water. Put on stove over high heat and bring water to a boil.
2. Add salt to boiling water.
3. Add spaghetti—a little at a time—and cook for 12 minutes. To see if spaghetti is cooked, use a fork to take out one piece. Cool off, then taste. If not tender, cook spaghetti for 2 or 3 more minutes and try another piece.
4. Immediately drain spaghetti in colander. Be careful of the steam. Pour away from you and pour slowly. Set spaghetti aside.
5. In small mixing bowl, combine eggs and Parmesan cheese. Mix well. Set aside.
6. Put spaghetti in large mixing bowl and add butter or margarine. Stir until melted. Pour egg and cheese mixture over spaghetti and mix well.
7. Apply non-stick cooking spray over bottom and around sides of 9-inch pie plate. Add spaghetti mixture. With fork, press spaghetti evenly around bottom and sides, forming a crust.

8. Preheat oven to 350°. Break up beef in 3-quart saucepan. On cutting board, chop onion into small pieces and add to beef. Sauté both over medium-high heat until meat is browned completely.

9. Turn off burner. Tip pan slightly and push beef mixture to one side. Remove all grease with mixing spoon.

10. Pour spaghetti sauce into pan with beef and stir until mixed. Spoon mixture evenly over spaghetti. Put into hot oven and bake for 20 minutes.

11. Place cheese slices on cutting board and cut from corner to corner so that each piece forms two triangles.

12. After baking pie for 20 minutes, remove from oven with potholders and arrange cheese on top of pie. Put back in oven for another 5 minutes or until cheese is melted. Serve hot.

Makes 6-8 servings.

COOKING TIPS

- Pasta won't stick together if you add one tablespoon of oil or vinegar to the boiling water before adding pasta.
- Cooking time varies depending on the type of pasta.
- Cooking pasta too long makes it soggy, and cooking it too little makes it chewy.
- Test pasta by biting a piece. The best pasta should be cooked through but taste a little rubbery.
- Practice a few times and it will come out just right.

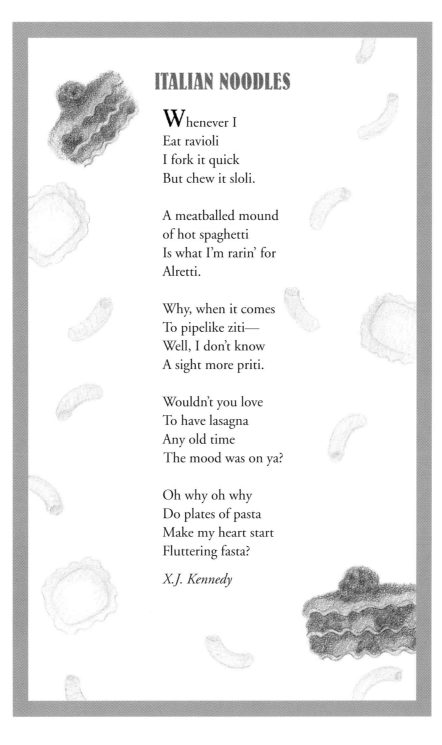

ITALIAN NOODLES

Whenever I
Eat ravioli
I fork it quick
But chew it sloli.

A meatballed mound
of hot spaghetti
Is what I'm rarin' for
Alretti.

Why, when it comes
To pipelike ziti—
Well, I don't know
A sight more priti.

Wouldn't you love
To have lasagna
Any old time
The mood was on ya?

Oh why oh why
Do plates of pasta
Make my heart start
Fluttering fasta?

X.J. Kennedy

"Italian Noodles" didn't begin in memory, but in pure fondness for words. (We never saw any pasta in our house when I was a kid, my father being a meat-and-potatoes fancier, so I didn't get entangled with spaghetti and other pasta until later.) In writing the poem, I was just trying to see how many names of noodles I could find rhymes for. The lines about lasagna sprang to mind first. Ravioli was the hardest pasta to rhyme. I never did find a rhyme for manicotti. Can you?

X.J. Kennedy

PASTA CHART

Pasta comes in many shapes. Below is a list of some of the popular varieties. Learn to identify your favorite choice, then ask for it when you order in a restaurant. You'll be a kid who knows how to use your noodle!

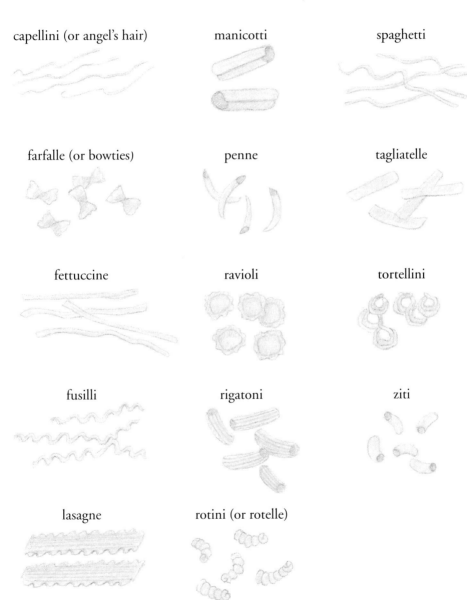

capellini (or angel's hair)	manicotti	spaghetti
farfalle (or bowties)	penne	tagliatelle
fettuccine	ravioli	tortellini
fusilli	rigatoni	ziti
lasagne	rotini (or rotelle)	

F was once a little fish
Fishy
Wishy
Squishy
Fishy
In a Dishy
Little Fish!

Edward Lear

There are eight basic ways to prepare fish: baking, broiling, sautéing, poaching, pan frying, oven frying, deep frying, and barbecuing. Almost any fish can be cooked by these methods.

If you use different seasonings, sauces, and flavored butters, you will have a rich variety of fish dinners!

Knowing how long to cook fish is essential to making it well. Cooking fish is like cooking an egg—the heat firms up the protein. Like an egg, fish becomes dry and tough when overcooked. Practice, and you'll be perfect at it in no time!

SESAME FISH

INGREDIENTS

1/2 cup chopped green onions
1/4 cup lemon juice
1/4 cup chopped parsley
2 pounds fish fillets
1/4 cup all-purpose flour
1/2 cup bread crumbs
1/4 cup sesame seeds
1 egg
2 tablespoons milk
salt and pepper
4 tablespoons butter or margarine
4 tablespoons salad oil
lemon relish (optional)

UTENSILS

3 small bowls
measuring cup
sharp knife
cutting board
measuring spoons
mixing spoon
wide frying pan
spatula
cooking glove
fork
plate

STEPS

1. In small bowl, combine green onions, lemon juice, and parsley. Set aside.
2. Rinse fish under cold water. Place on cutting board. Cut into bite-sized pieces.
3. Place flour on plate. Roll pieces of fish in flour until well coated.
4. In another small bowl, combine bread crumbs and sesame seeds.
5. In third small bowl, mix egg and milk.
6. Dip fish pieces into egg mixture and shake off excess. Then dip in crumb mixture and shake off excess. Sprinkle salt and pepper to taste.
7. In frying pan, melt 2 tablespoons of butter or margarine and 2 table-spoons of oil over medium heat.
8. When mixture sizzles, add fish without overcrowding pan. Cook 8-10 minutes, turning once with spatula or fork. Fish should be white when poked with fork. Use cooking glove to protect you from spattering grease.
9. Transfer cooked fish to a plate and cover to keep warm. Cook remaining fish, adding butter or oil as needed.
10. Spoon lemon relish over fish if desired.

Makes 4-6 servings.

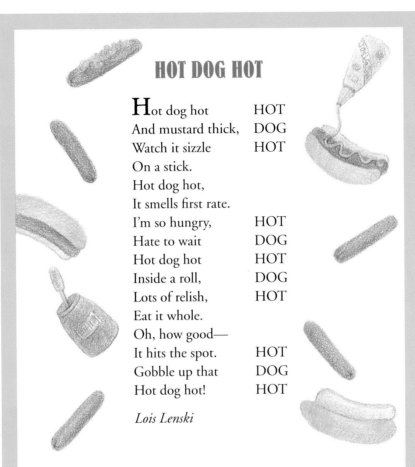

HOT DOG HOT

Hot dog hot	HOT
And mustard thick,	DOG
Watch it sizzle	HOT
On a stick.	
Hot dog hot,	
It smells first rate.	
I'm so hungry,	HOT
Hate to wait	DOG
Hot dog hot	HOT
Inside a roll,	DOG
Lots of relish,	HOT
Eat it whole.	
Oh, how good—	
It hits the spot.	HOT
Gobble up that	DOG
Hot dog hot!	HOT

Lois Lenski

HOW THE HOT DOG GOT ITS BUN

Sometime in the 1880s, a peddler in St. Louis who sold sausages in the street gave out white gloves to wear while eating the sausages so that customers wouldn't burn their hands. Although business was good, the peddler lost money because everyone kept walking off with his gloves. One night the peddler's wife suggested that he sell the sausages inside a bun so that no one would burn their hands. That's how the hot dog got its bun!

ROUND HOT DOGS

INGREDIENTS

water
4 hot dogs
4 round hamburger buns
1 can of baked beans

UTENSILS

2 2-quart saucepans—one
    with top
sharp knife
aluminum foil
can opener
wooden spoon
fork
potholders

STEPS

1. Preheat oven to 250°. Fill one saucepan halfway with water and place on medium-high heat. Bring to a boil.
2. Make cuts in hot dogs 1/2 inch apart, but don't cut all the way through.
3. Place hot dogs in saucepan of boiling water for 7 minutes. Cover.
4. While hot dogs are cooking, wrap hamburger buns in aluminum foil and place in oven for 10 minutes or until warm.
5. Open can of baked beans.* Spoon contents of can into second saucepan. Cook until hot, stirring occasionally with wooden spoon.
6. When hot dogs have cooked, remove saucepan from heat with potholders. Remove hot dogs from boiling water with fork and place on buns. Be careful of steam. Hot dogs will be curled up.
7. Add beans to center and cover with top of bun.

Makes 4 servings.

*Other things you can put inside: sauerkraut, pizza sauce and cheese, mustard, ketchup, relish. What else can you think of? Come up with your own clever concoction.

41

SIDE ORDERS

No main course is complete by itself. Try one of the suggestions mentioned on the next few pages. Each recipe goes with a sandwich or a hot evening meal, and you can create them in a snap!

The poems in this section are more than side orders! Keep them on the front burner—a hot spot for any time of day.

RAW CARROTS

Raw carrots taste
Cool and hard,
Like some crisp metal.

Horses are
Fond of them,
Crunching up

The red gold
With much wet
Juice and noise.

Carrots must taste
To horses
As they do to us.

Valerie Worth

At the age of eleven or twelve I was crazy about horses. On Saturday mornings I would set off for the local stables, taking along a few lumps of sugar and a carrot for my favorite horse. But sometimes on the way I couldn't help taking a bite of carrot, and then another bite—and by the time I got there, only a last stubby inch of it would be left for the horse!

Valerie Worth

CRUNCHY SALAD

INGREDIENTS

2 carrots
1 stalk of celery
2 apples
1/2 cup raisins
1 teaspoon lemon juice
1/4 teaspoon salt
1/2 cup yogurt or sour cream
lettuce

UTENSILS

paring knife
vegetable peeler
grater
large mixing bowl
measuring cup
measuring spoons

STEPS

1. Wash carrots, celery, and apples.
2. Cut off ends of carrots, peel, then grate. Put in large mixing bowl.
3. Cut out core of apples. Cut the rest into small bite-sized pieces. Add to large mixing bowl.
4. Cut celery into small pieces and put in bowl.
5. Add raisins.
6. Sprinkle with lemon juice and salt.
7. Stir in yogurt or sour cream.
8. Serve on large lettuce leaves.

Makes 4 servings.

A cheese that was aged and gray
Was walking and talking one day.
Said the cheese, "Kindly note
My mama was a goat
And I'm made out of curds by the whey."

Anonymous

Cheesemaking begins with milk—from any milk-producing animal—and the separation of curds (solid matter) from whey (liquid portion).

There's a legend that cheese was discovered by a shepherd boy around 4000 B.C. One day, while the boy was on his rounds, he left his milk pouch in the sun. When he came back for a drink, he found a surprise—cheese in his milk pouch! The heat had combined with the enzymes, coagulating the milk. Cheese had been created.

* * * * * * * * * *

I eat my peas with honey;
I've done it all my life.
It makes the peas taste funny,
But it keeps them on the knife.

Anonymous

PEAS WITH CHEESE

INGREDIENTS

1 10-ounce package frozen peas
2 tablespoons water
2 tablespoons butter or margarine
2 tablespoons all-purpose flour
1 cup milk
1/2 cup cheddar or muenster
   cheese, grated

UTENSILS

2 1-quart saucepans
measuring spoons
wooden spoons (one with long
   handle)
measuring cup
small baking dish
potholders

STEPS

1. Preheat oven to 350°.
2. Place frozen peas in 1-quart saucepan. Add 2 tablespoons of water. Cover. Put over high heat and steam for about 5 minutes. Stir once or twice. Take pan off stove and set aside.
3. Melt butter or margarine in a small saucepan. Add flour and mix. Stir with wooden spoon for a few minutes over medium-low heat until smooth.
4. Add milk to butter mixture. The mixture will begin to get thick and creamy in about 8-10 minutes. Stir occasionally.
5. Add grated cheese to butter mixture and stir until cheese melts.
6. Pour peas into baking dish. Add cheese sauce and stir together carefully.
7. Place dish in oven and bake uncovered at 350° for 30-35 minutes or until cheese forms crusty top.

Makes 2-4 servings.

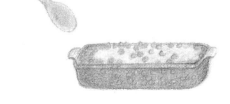

They every one have eyes, but not one of them can see,
You find them every size. They are good as they can be.
You can dig them in a field, in a hill they hide away.
You will eat them just at noon, almost any day!

(Potatoes)

Unknown

Did you know? . . . When Hollywood moviemakers need to create a scene with falling snow and the weather is clear, they sometimes use instant mashed potato flakes as snow!

POTATO FLAT

INGREDIENTS

4-5 medium potatoes
1 medium onion
4 tablespoons butter or margarine
salt and pepper (optional)
sour cream and chives (optional)

UTENSILS

vegetable peeler
saucepan
fork
cutting board
paring knife
large skillet
medium bowl
spatula
flat serving plate
potholders

STEPS

1. Peel and rinse off potatoes. Cut into quarters and put in saucepan. Cover with cold water and bring to a boil over medium heat.
2. Cook until potatoes are soft when poked with a fork, approximately 25 minutes. Take off stove, drain, and let cool.
3. Place onion on cutting board and chop into small pieces. Add 3 tablespoons of butter or margarine to skillet and let melt on low heat. Then gently add onion pieces and cook on medium-high heat until browned.
4. Mash cooled potatoes with fork on cutting board until soft.
5. In medium mixing bowl, stir onion and potatoes together. Add salt and pepper, if desired. Stir together.
6. Add remaining butter or margarine to skillet, making sure the bottom and sides of pan are covered evenly.
7. Put potato and onion mixture into skillet and cook on stove over low heat for 25 minutes, turning pan around every few minutes.
8. When potatoes are ready, remove skillet from heat. Lay a flat serving plate upside down over skillet, holding one hand over middle of plate with potholder in between. Carefully turn both over together so that potato cake falls into plate right side up. Set plate on counter and remove pan. If you need assistance, ask an older person to help you with this.
9. Cut as you would a pie or pizza. Add sour cream and chives if desired.

Serves 4-6.

TOMATO TIME

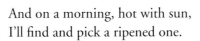

On a summer vine, and low,
The fat tomatoes burst and grow;

A green, a pink, a yellow head
Will soon be warm and shiny red;

And on a morning, hot with sun,
I'll find and pick a ripened one.

Warm juice and seeds beneath the skin—
I'll shut my eyes when I bite in.

Myra Cohn Livingston

"Tomato Time" was written a few days after I had picked tomatoes off the vine for the first time in my life. My husband and I were invited to a swimming party . . . and there was a huge tomato vine on the property. I had somehow never been around tomatoes. It was a glorious discovery . . . which may partially explain my excitement over picking a warm, fresh, ripe tomato, which still remains one of my favorite foods and which I always grow in my own garden.

Myra Cohn Livingston

EASY TOMATO SOUP

INGREDIENTS

1 cup water
1 beef bouillon cube
1 cup tomato juice
1 teaspoon basil

UTENSILS

measuring cup
2-quart saucepan
potholder
measuring spoons
wooden spoon

STEPS

1. Pour one cup of water into saucepan and put saucepan on stove over high heat. Bring to boil.
2. Remove saucepan from heat. Add bouillon cube to boiling water and stir with wooden spoon until dissolved.
3. Stir in tomato juice and basil.
4. Return saucepan to stove on medium heat until soup is hot.
5. Serve warm.

Makes 2 servings.

SWEET ENDINGS

If you want something sweet to complete your meal, crunch into an apple and taste its cold splash. Bite into an orange or banana and feel the sweetness trickle down your throat. Reach into a cookie jar and pull out a treat. Cut a slice of freshly baked cake.

Poems are sweet. They are a treat. Tangy and delicious, too. Make each dessert and each poem last as long as you can. Both are morsels worth savoring.

ORANGES

Hang an orange on a tree
You have a Christmas ball;
Throw an orange to a friend
You have an orange ball;
Toss an orange in the air
You have a little sun;
Put an orange on your plate
Have your breakfast . . .
Don't be late!

Patricia Hubbell

Oranges! Aren't they beautiful! Painters paint them, poets write about them, everyone (just about) eats them. I wrote the poem "Oranges" one day when I was thinking about the different things an orange could be used for . . . a Christmas ornament . . . a ball . . . even a little sun.

One year when I was little, we had a Christmas tree trimmed just with apples and popcorn balls. Apples, all over, tied with red ribbons. So I guess it seemed natural to me that you might have a tree trimmed with oranges.

Patricia Hubbell

IF I WERE AN APPLE

If I were an apple
  And grew on a tree,
I'd ripen and fall
  On a nice boy like me.

I wouldn't stay high,
  Giving nobody joy.
I'd drop to the ground
  And say "Eat me, my boy!"

Old Rhyme

FIVE APPLE VARIETIES

MᴄIɴᴛᴏꜱʜ—This apple has red skin. It's sweet and tender—good for eating and for making applesauce.

Rᴇᴅ Dᴇʟɪᴄɪᴏᴜꜱ—This apple has bright red skin and five knobs at the bottom. It's good for eating.

Gᴏʟᴅᴇɴ Dᴇʟɪᴄɪᴏᴜꜱ—This apple has a bright golden skin. It's firm and crisp—good for cooking or eating for dessert.

Sᴘᴀʀᴛᴀɴ—This apple is red with white dots on the skin. It's medium-sized and good for eating and cooking.

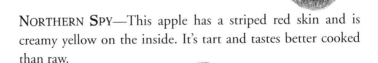

Nᴏʀᴛʜᴇʀɴ Sᴘʏ—This apple has a striped red skin and is creamy yellow on the inside. It's tart and tastes better cooked than raw.

APPLE CREAM

INGREDIENTS

1 cup heavy cream
1 cup cinnamon applesauce
1 tablespoon honey
2 1/2 tablespoons lemon juice
3/4 teaspoon cinnamon
1/2 teaspoon sugar
mint leaf (optional)
apple (optional)

UTENSILS

2 mixing bowls
mixing spoon
measuring cup
measuring spoons
hand beater or hand-held electric mixer
rubber scraper
small dessert dishes or parfait glasses
small bowl
mixing spoon
grater (optional)

STEPS

1. Chill cream, mixing bowl, and beaters by placing in refrigerator for 30 minutes.
2. In another mixing bowl, add applesauce, honey, lemon juice, and 1/4 teaspoon cinnamon. Mix well.
3. Put cream in chilled mixing bowl. Beat until cream is thick and stands up when you lift out beaters. Use medium-high speed for electric mixer.
4. Carefully pour whipping cream into applesauce mixture. Scrape excess from bowl with rubber scraper.
5. Pour into dessert dishes or parfait glasses.
6. Mix sugar and remaining cinnamon in small bowl and sprinkle on top of individual portions.
7. For garnish, add piece of mint leaf or spoonful of grated apple on top of individual portions.

BANANAS AND CREAM

Bananas and cream,
Bananas and cream:
All we could say was
Bananas and cream.

We couldn't say fruit,
We wouldn't say cow,
We didn't say sugar—
We don't say it now.

Bananas and cream,
Bananas and cream,
All we could shout was
Bananas and cream.

We didn't say why,
We didn't say how;
We forgot it was fruit,
We forgot the old cow;
We never said sugar,
We only said WOW!

David McCord

BANANA MOUSE

INGREDIENTS

banana
lemon juice
2 sliced almond pieces
2 semisweet chocolate morsels or
   2 raisins
1 whole almond or peanut
1 tablespoon soft-style cream cheese
1 piece uncooked spaghetti
1 2-inch piece thin black licorice

UTENSILS

paring knife
pastry brush
measuring spoon

STEPS

1. Cut a 2-inch piece of banana.
2. Spread lemon juice over banana with pastry brush. Let dry.
3. Press two sliced almond pieces into top of banana to make ears.
4. Spread back of chocolate morsels or raisins with cream cheese and press onto banana to make eyes.
5. Spread back of almond or peanut with cream cheese and press onto banana to make nose.
6. Break spaghetti into 1-inch pieces and push into banana to make whiskers.
7. Push licorice into back of banana to make tail.

Makes 1 mouse.

BIRTHDAY CAKE

If little mice have birthdays
(and I suppose they do)

And have a family party
(and guests invited too)

And have a cake with candles
(it would be rather small)

I bet a birthday CHEESE cake
would please them most of all.

Aileen Fisher

CHOCOLATE SURPRISE MINI-CAKES

INGREDIENTS

Filling

3 ounces cream cheese, softened

1/4 cup sugar

1/2 teaspoon vanilla

Cake Portion

2/3 cup all-purpose, pre-sifted flour

1/4 cup unsweetened cocoa powder

1 teaspoon baking powder

1/4 cup sugar

1/4 cup butter or margarine, softened

1 large egg

1/2 teaspoon vanilla

1/2 cup milk

UTENSILS

12 paper bake cups

muffin pan

measuring cup

measuring spoons

2 small mixing bowls

sifter

medium mixing bowl

3 mixing spoons

potholders

STEPS

1. Preheat oven to 375°. Put 12 paper bake cups into muffin pan.
2. To make filling, combine cream cheese, sugar, and vanilla in small bowl. Mix well and set aside.
3. To make cake portion, sift flour, then combine with cocoa and baking powder in separate small bowl. Mix well.
4. In medium bowl, mix sugar and butter until fluffy. Stir in egg and vanilla. Mix well.
5. Add half of flour mixture to butter mixture. Stir. Slowly stir in milk until smooth. Add rest of flour mixture. Stir until smooth.
6. Spoon 1 tablespoon of cake batter into each bake cup. Add cheese filling on top of batter in each cup. Spoon 1 tablespoon of cake batter on top of cheese filling.
7. Put muffin pan into oven. Bake for 20 minutes. Remove with potholders and let cool.

Makes 12 mini-cakes.

COOKIE CUTTERS

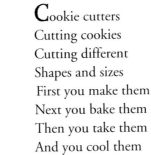

Cookie cutters
Cutting cookies
Cutting different
Shapes and sizes
First you make them
Next you bake them
Then you take them
And you cool them
And . . .
That's weird.
They've disappeared!

Mary Ann Hoberman

We all know how hard it is to keep home-baked cookies around.

Mary Ann Hoberman

OATMEAL-RAISIN COOKIES

INGREDIENTS

1 stick butter or margarine
2/3 cup brown sugar
1/3 cup granulated sugar
1 egg
1 teaspoon vanilla
1 tablespoon milk
1 cup all-purpose flour
1/2 teaspoon baking soda
1/2 teaspoon baking powder
1/2 teaspoon salt
1 cup rolled oats
1/2 cup raisins
butter or margarine
    (to grease cookie sheet) or
    non-stick cooking spray

UTENSILS

small skillet
wooden spoon
mixing spoon
small bowls
measuring spoons
measuring cup
cookie sheet
potholders
spatula
large plate

STEPS

1. Preheat oven to 350°.
2. Melt butter in skillet over low heat. Add sugars and mix with wooden spoon until smooth. Take skillet off stove and set aside.
3. Break egg into small bowl and mix in vanilla and milk.
4. In another small bowl, mix flour, baking soda, baking powder, and salt.
5. Combine egg and butter mixtures and mix well. Add flour mixture. Stir until smooth.
6. Add oats and raisins. Mix well.
7. Spoon cookie dough 2 inches apart on well-greased or sprayed cookie sheet and bake for 10 minutes or until golden brown. Take out of oven with potholders and let cookies cool on cookie sheet.
8. Use spatula to scoop cookies onto large plate.

Makes 2-3 dozen cookies.

ACKNOWLEDGMENTS

Every possible effort has been made to trace the ownership of each poem included in PEAS AND HONEY. If any errors or omissions have occurred, corrections will be made in subsequent printings, provided the publisher is notified of their existence.

Permission to reprint copyrighted poems is gratefully acknowledged to the following:

Atheneum Publishers for "Oranges" from THE APPLE VENDOR'S FAIR by Patricia Hubbell. Copyright © 1963, and renewed 1991, by Patricia Hubbell. Reprinted with permission of Atheneum Publishers, an imprint of Macmillan Publishing Company.

Bantam Books for "If the Moon Were Made of Cheese," from the BUTTERFLY JAR by Jeff Moss. Copyright © 1989 by Jeff Moss. Used by permission of Bantam Books, a division of Bantam Doubleday Dell Publishing Group, Inc.

Farrar, Straus & Giroux, Inc., for "Raw Carrots" from SMALL POEMS by Valerie Worth. Copyright © 1972 by Valerie Worth. Reprinted by permission of Farrar, Straus & Giroux, Inc.

Aileen Fisher for "An Egg" from I WONDER HOW, I WONDER WHY. Copyright © 1962, Abelard Schuman, Ltd. Copyright renewed; and for "Muffins" from UP THE WINDY HILL. Copyright © 1953, Abelard Press/NY. Copyright renewed; and for "Birthday Cake" from RUNNY DAYS, SUNNY DAYS. Copyright © 1958. Copyright renewed.

HarperCollins Publishers Ltd. for "If You're No Good at Cooking" from RABBITING ON by Kit Wright. Reprinted by permission of HarperCollins Publishers Ltd.

Steven Kroll for "The Perfect Turkey Sandwich." Copyright © 1977 by Steven Kroll. Reprinted by permission of the author.

The Lois Lenski Covey Foundation for "Hot Dog Hot" from CITY POEMS. Copyright © 1971 by Lois Lenski; and "More Pancakes" from THE LIFE I LIVE. Copyright © 1965 by Lois Lenski. Reprinted with permission.

Little, Brown and Company for "Bananas and Cream" and "Peanut Butter" (Part 4 of "From the Kitchen: Ten Poems") from ONE AT A TIME by David McCord. Copyright © 1961, 1962, 1974 by David McCord. First appeared in *Yankee Magazine*. Reprinted by permission of Little, Brown and Company.

Gina Maccoby Literary Agency for "Cookie Cutters" from NUTS TO YOU AND NUTS TO ME. Copyright © 1974 by Mary Ann Hoberman and for "Yellow Butter" from YELLOW BUTTER PURPLE JELLY RED JAM BLACK BREAD. Copyright © 1981 by Mary Ann Hoberman.

Margaret K. McElderry Books for "Italian Noodles" (expanded version of "Lasagna") from GHASTLIES, GOOPS & PINCUSHIONS by X.J. Kennedy. Copyright © 1979, 1989 by X.J. Kennedy. Reprinted with permission of Margaret K. McElderry Books, an imprint of Macmillan Publishing Company.

William Morrow & Company, Inc., for "Spaghetti! Spaghetti!" from RAINY RAINY SATURDAY. Copyright © 1980 by Jack Prelutsky. Reprinted by permission of William Morrow & Company, Inc., Publishers, New York.

Marian Reiner for "Tomato Time" from A SONG I SANG TO YOU by Myra Cohn Livingston. Copyright © 1984, 1969, 1967, 1965, 1959, 1958 by Myra Cohn Livingston. Reprinted by permission of Marian Reiner for the author.

AUTHOR INDEX

RECIPE INDEX

TITLE AND FIRST LINE INDEX